The House of Grana Padano

MEG POKRASS AND JEFF FRIEDMAN

Pelekinesis

The House of Grana Padano by Meg Pokrass and Jeff Friedman
ISBN: 978-1-949790-49-8
eISBN: 978-1-949790-50-4

Copyright © 2022 Meg Pokrass and Jeff Friedman.
All rights reserved.

Cover art by Meg Pokrass and Mark Givens
Layout and book design by Mark Givens

First Pelekinesis Printing 2022

For information:
Pelekinesis, 112 Harvard Ave #65, Claremont, CA 91711 USA

Library of Congress Cataloging-in-Publication Data

Names: Pokrass, Meg, author. | Friedman, Jeff, author.
Title: The house of Grana Padano / Meg Pokrass and Jeff Friedman.
Description: Claremont, CA : Pelekinesis, [2022] | Summary: "The House of
  Grana Padano is a collection of tragi-comic, fabulist microfiction by
  two modern masters of the form, each story a world unto itself"--
  Provided by publisher.
Identifiers: LCCN 2022003600 (print) | LCCN 2022003601 (ebook) | ISBN
  9781949790498 (paperback) | ISBN 9781949790504 (epub)
Subjects: LCGFT: Flash fiction.
Classification: LCC PS3616.O5565 H68 2022 (print) | LCC PS3616.O5565
  (ebook) | DDC 813/.6--dc23/eng/20220208
LC record available at https://lccn.loc.gov/2022003600
LC ebook record available at https://lccn.loc.gov/2022003601

Pelekinesis
www.pelekinesis.com

The House of Grana Padano

A Collection of Fabulist Microfiction

Meg Pokrass & Jeff Friedman

Acknowledgments

Our thanks to the editors of the following publications in which these fabulist microfictions first appeared:

American Journal of Poetry: "Broken Man"

Café Irreal: "Quaking," "The Salesman Gets Stoned," and "Dead Bugs and Lovers"

Contrary: "Rainmakers," "Sold," "My Father the Salesman," and "Bad Day for the Salesman"

Daily Drunk: "Pet Loss"

Emery's Online: "Adam's Rib"

Fifty-Word Story: "Pet Loss"

Fort Nightly Review: "Mime Love Story"

Hole in the Head Review: "Along Comes Mary" and "The Salesman Has a Vision"

MacQueen's Quinterly: Mistaking One Cheese for Another," "The Not So Invisible Ex," and "The Grana Padano House of Wedgewood"

Midway Journal: "Dad with Porpoise"

New World Writing: The Weak Man in the Circus," "Out of Touch," and "Family Sorcerer"

Odd Magazine: "Near Collision on Main Street"

On the Seawall: "The Salesman Gets a Suit," "Something Special," "My Mother The Realtor," and "The Salesman Grows Sad"

Pangyrus: "Gifted Sister," "Owl Eyes," and "Her Blue Period"

Plume: "Fatherless Daughter" and "What You Can't Fix"

Right Hand Pointing: "Memories of Motown"

Unbroken: "Out of the Hat" and "Snapping Turtle"

Vox Populi: "Wig Story"

Whale Road Review: "My Circus Grandmother"

Wigleaf: "Picking Up the Moose"

"Sneaker Wave" was initially published under the title of "The Weeki Waatchi Mermaid" in *Fictive Dream.*

"As melancholy is sadness that has taken on lightness, so humor is comedy that has lost its bodily weight ... It casts doubt on the self, on the world, and on the whole network of relationships that are at stake."

—Italo Calvino

Contents

Section 1
The Sales Force

Bad Day for the Salesman 15
The Cost of the Cat..16
My Mother the Realtor 17
My Father the Salesman 18
The Diet-Book Salesman 19
The Salesman Gets a Suit...20
Something Special 21
Rainmakers...22
Sold...23
The Salesman Grows Sad..24
Who Sold You This? 25
The Salesman Has a Vision 26
The Salesman Gets Stoned 27

Section 2
The Circus Comes to Town

The Weak Man in the Circus 31
Thanksgiving for a Diner Clown.....................................32
Nightshade 33
Eddie at Home 35
My Circus Grandmother 36
The Former Bearded Lady in the Circus........................37
The Saddest Woman on Earth 38
Goldfish Skin..39
Kissing Booth...41
Almost Anything 42
Some Girls Swallow the Concept of Hell.......................43
Return of the Dead Magician...45
The Angel Act...46
The Quiet Woman 47
Last Bow of the Clown..48

Section 3
Motown and More

Memories of Motown 51
Looking for Motown..52
Along Comes Mary 53
What Is It About Mary...54
Broken Man 55
Picking Up the Moose..56
Where Motown Lives...57
Broken Man, Broken Woman 58
Cramped Love...59
The Death of Motown 60
Walking Away from Motown..61

Section 4
Messing with Love

What You Can't Fix 65
Out of Touch 66
Flying Off...67
Fish Story 68
Moose Stand Off 69
The Charm of the Foul-Mouthed Wife 70
Hall of Masks 71
The End of her Blue Period 72
Heading toward Vegas 73
Betrayal 74
Dusk 75
Birds Don't Like You 76
Snow Wonder...77
Quiet 78
Mime Love...79
Pet Loss 80

Section 5
Curse of the Family

Owl Eyes 85
Abandoned Father 86
In Childhood 87
Gifted Sister 88
Searching for the Bearded Dragon 89
Father Obscura 90
Mom In the Kitchen 91
Wig 92
Trolllikeness 94
Menopausal Mother 95
Redundancy 97
Kiss-Monger 98
Snapping Turtle 99
House Full of Dust 100
Nose Job 101
A Birthday Wish 102
Family Sorcerer 103
Fatherless Daughters 105

Section 6
House of Grana Padano

The Grana Padano House of Wedgewood 109
The Smell of the Ex 110
The Nervous Little Wife 111
Mistaking One Cheese for Another 112
Near Collision on Main Street 113
Kissing Grana Padano 114
It Wasn't Really Blue 115
Didn't We See Her? 116
Like 117

Section 7
Cognac Dream

Wolf Hybrids 121
Cognac Dream 123
Catching the Future... 124
Sneaker Wave 125
Quaking 126
Dad With Porpoise.. 127
No Rescue... 128
Looking for a Light... 129
Dream Retrieval.. 130
Snail Women 131
Dead Bugs and Lovers 133
Out of the Hat 134

Section 1

The Sales Force

Bad Day for the Salesman

The salesman headed home after another day without a sale. The sun was dissolving in the sky, and the sky leaned down dangerously close to the trees. The birds were calling to each other, but he couldn't identify any of them. Nor could he identify the birds he saw, except the crow walking over a lawn, scavenging for food. He shifted his case with all his goods from hand to hand as it had grown too heavy hours ago. He arrived home, turned the key in the lock and opened the door, but the chain was on. He knocked and shouted for his wife, who took her time getting to him. "You again?" she said. He took out a basting brush to give her. She shook her head. "What do I want with a basting brush? I never grill." He opened his case and removed his best boar-bristle brush, the one with the silver handle. "Put it back," she said. "I don't use that kind of brush. It catches and tugs my hair." He reached his hand in to unchain the chain, but he got nowhere with it. "Is that the best you can do?" she asked. "You're in the wrong profession." Then before he could give her another pitch, she shut the door, double clicking the locks.

The Cost of the Cat

The saleswoman lives in a broken-down apartment with an old cat she loves too much. She has a part-time boyfriend, who reminds her that it's the weekend. "You're working too hard," he says repeatedly. "How will I pay for her medical bills?" she asks. You can't keep her," he says, "if you can't afford her. This only makes sense." She doesn't want to make sense. She needs her cat and isn't sure about her boyfriend. "Will you pay for my vet bills when I'm old?" she says and laughs as if she is joking. She knows how to sell with her nut-brown eyes. She looks up at her boyfriend, touches his wrist and smiles as if she knows just what he needs. She smells fish on his breath and in the air of his condo, because he always eats fish. "It's healthy for the heart," he says. Her cat smells more human. Also, he hasn't asked her to move in, though they've been together for years. *Why is he hanging around?* She wonders. She smiles the same way at her clients, eyes aimed at their faces. Until she turned forty, they wanted whatever she sold.

My Mother the Realtor

Hiding from men like a gorgeous nun, my divorced mother was wedded to her spotless car. She sold houses to newly married couples who were loaded with cash, lucky out-of-town buyers, who took in everything she said about real estate in California as though hypnotized by her beautiful but impractical dresses. She drove them from posh neighborhood to posh neighborhood and talked to them about dreams and possibilities, about living in the silks of luxury and standing with their cocktails on the lovely verandas as they leaned toward the hills, talked to them about the exotic birds that fly out of the twilight and change the lives of everyone who sees them. "Beautiful people become beautiful by living in these houses," she would say. At home, late in the evening, she'd tell me, "The business is drying up." And I learned how to assure her that it wasn't, learned how to sell her back her own dream that the future was ours.

My Father the Salesman

In his will, my father left me only an envelope filled with Kennedy half dollars. I searched his drawers and closets, but never found them. "Your father really knew how to live it up," my mother would say regretfully. She would drink vodka martinis dry, her eyes froggy. "He spent twice what he made," she said, "but he could sell a wolf a double-breasted suit, a snake a pair of new loafers, a frog a suede vest." Unfortunately, that market dried up as he got older. Stumbling around with a hangover one morning, my father plugged in the toaster oven while the dishwasher was running and blew out the power in the whole building. My mother knocked on each door to apologize to the neighbors, but not one of them would answer. "Your father couldn't fix anything around the house," my mother would say, "but he certainly knew how to break things." Only once, she told me how my father was a very special kisser. "His lips were so hot they could melt an ice cube."

The Diet-Book Salesman

He sold diet books to war widows and made a small fortune. He'd knock on doors with the book in hand. "Guaranteed success," he said when they looked at him through the partially opened door. Charmed by his compassionate smile and the possibilities inherent in weight loss, the women would remove the chain and let him in. "You can be even more beautiful; it's simple," he would say, fanning the pages of an overpriced book. He placed it in their hands to let them feel the lightness of it. "You'll lose 10 pounds just by reading the introduction." Worked every time. Then the market dried up. Either the widows had remarried or died off. Single women didn't even open their doors, and married women cursed him for implying they were overweight. He was broke, walking through his territory with a box of old books. The sun glared in his eyes. His feet felt the pavement through the thinning soles of his shoes.

The Salesman Gets a Suit

My father walks into a clothing store. "Sell me a suit," he says to a thin bald-headed man. Without even looking, the bald-headed man pulls a blue silk suit off the rack. "This suit is made for you," he says holding the hanger in his right hand and letting the pant legs drape over his arm. "Just feel it." My father brushes it gently with his fingers as though smoothing out the curls of his own hair. "I'm a salesman too," he says. "I knew it," the bald-headed man says. "I could tell the minute you entered the store." The suit is shiny like the lobby in a posh hotel, shiny like a brand new Cadillac parked in the car dealer's window. My father takes it into the dressing room, and when he comes out, the suit swells with his plump belly. The sleeves of the jacket swallow his hands. The pants legs sweep the floor. He looks short and fat, lost in cloth. "This suit makes you look like a whole new man, like someone ready to make a killing," the bald-headed man says and leads him to the mirror. In the mirror, the suit shapes itself to his body, fits him to a tee. In the mirror, he's as graceful as a shadow, as light on his feet as a cool breeze rustling his pant legs. He leans forward as if telling the suit a secret. He smiles, and the suit smiles back.

Something Special

After returning from a two-week sales trip one Friday evening, my father swept through the door like a gust of leaves and dust, a wind blowing through the rooms of our apartment. He heaved his suitcases onto his bed and unloaded his samples first, hanging them in the closet, and then his wilted shirts and pants. "Don't make a mess," my mother said—too late. He always made a mess. Debris was scattered on the floor, and she began sweeping around him with a broom she kept handy in their bedroom closet. Out of the suitcase, my father lifted a tiny bronze-colored roulette wheel. "I bought this for you," he said. "It's one of a kind." It looked like something that might have come from a Crackerjack box. I stared at it for a moment and then he placed it in my hand. "Don't break it." He had promised to bring home something really special, an early Chanukah gift. I didn't hide my disappointment. He laughed. "Here's your real gift." From his pocket, he plucked a shiny coin, larger than a quarter. "Do you know what this is?" he asked. "A Kennedy half-dollar," I answered. I reached for it, knowing I could buy ten packs of baseball cards or ten Nestle Crunches with it, but he closed his palm on the coin. "Not so fast. I'll keep it for you," he said. "Someday, it'll be worth something."

Rainmakers

Salespeople are victims of their products. The numbers around which they orbit are like meteor showers. They lie down in bed and think about the way people buy things from them, how easy it has always been. They wonder, *why am I slick?* They lie very still with their thoughts. This is how they learn to be rainmakers, letting the drops fall from the clouds they conjure, the drops that never touch them.

Sold

A saleswoman and her customer meet in an alley. They kiss as if they already know each other. "Your skin still smells like easy money," he whispers, running his hand through her hair. "Damn right it does," she says, nuzzling her nose against his wool coat. "Beautiful, soft wool," she says. "Where did you buy it?" "What a great question," he says. "From you, of course."

She can't remember ever having sold anyone a coat. But he pulls her in right up against his pacemaker, so she can feel the cold warmth of his heart and hear what makes him tick.

The Salesman Grows Sad

How can he survive if everyone is staring at their television screens instead of answering the door when he rings or knocks? How can he show them the miracle Dust, Clean and Wax that will clean the stains off everything without leaving behind a film or another stain? How can he show them the beauty of his boar-bristle brushes? and the crumb roller that is used on the tabletops and tablecloths in all the best restaurants? He thinks hard. Maybe he could hold up a sign in their windows that says in big bold letters, "Free Green Basting Brush—Just for Opening Your Door." Who doesn't want a good basting brush? The crows follow him up and down the block. He throws a free basting brush at them, but it sails over their heads. They laugh at him. For all he knows, he might be a crow himself. He opens his wings and flaps rapidly. And now he imagines flying into the trees with his suitcase, planting himself on a branch. But when he looks down, he's standing in front of someone's door, knocking louder and louder.

Who Sold You This?

After I cleaned the mirror, she pointed to three streaks. "I'm not so good with glass," I said. "That's why you need a more effective cleaner," she said. I was using water on a paper towel. She opened the cabinet under the bathroom sink and pulled out a bottle of bright green liquid. "Easy On the Eyes," the label read. "Who sold you this?" I asked. "No one," she answered. She sprayed it on the window and wiped it off. The streaks were gone, and the glass was almost invisible. "I've just always used it, because I like to see myself clearly." "I guess I prefer seeing myself in a haze or mist," I said and laughed. But next to her, I looked dazed and small.

"Not good enough," she said, having spotted a smear. She sprayed and wiped the mirror again. Now it was so clean and bright her smile was blinding, but I had disappeared.

The Salesman Has a Vision

Each night I sat on the porch and wished to regain my lost motivation, my desire to sell others what they don't need. Each night I wondered, how much longer can I go without any sales? Weeks turned into months. Then one night the dust rose above the roofs. I climbed the hill behind my house and looked down on a narrow road that circled the hill. The dust rose as if a line of people were following each other single file around and around. But the road was empty, and the only light came from the moon. There was not even a trace of wind. The next day, I dropped my old line of goods and instead began selling emptiness, drawers with nothing in them, wind-up dolls that don't speak, music boxes that play music no one can hear, wrapped packages of the lights from fireflies, and boxes of blessings from the pockets of invisible gods.

The Salesman Gets Stoned

The salesman wore pants that billowed in the wind. Without a single sale for the day, he carried his briefcase up the block determined to get to the next neighborhood. On the way, he saluted a crow sitting on the stone post that led to a small graveyard, and the crow saluted him back. As he walked beside the graveyard, ghosts were waving their bony arms as they sat in front of the headstones and passed a joint. One held it up as a signal for him to come over. The salesman smiled and approached the ghosts. "You're ghosts. How come I can see you in broad daylight?" "We're not that kind of ghosts," one answered and handed him a joint. "What's in the case?" another ghost asked. "My line of goods," he answered and took a deep pull on the joint and after a long moment, let out the smoke. He took another and then another and passed on the joint. "Maybe you should sit down, Brother," one ghost said. "You're looking a little like a ghost." Now he was stoned, and the ghosts didn't look so much like ghosts, more like the gray-faced men he had seen sitting on benches in town. He set out for his territory again, but the road curved in front of and behind him. And he kept turning.

Section 2

The Circus Comes to Town

The Weak Man in the Circus

I live on a diet of air particles and gnats, enough to keep me awake, but not enough to give me the strength to walk outside or even to lift a glass of water to my lips. For if I could do that, I would lose my living. Each day, the boisterous crowd clamors inside my tent eager to see me attempt my famous feats. I start with hoisting a book, but my skinny arms can't hold it up for even a second, so it falls on the ground. Then I rise slowly with Selena, my lover and assistant, at my side, holding me up as I take a step or two. Next, I might flex my arm to show off my very small hump of a bicep and my bony elbows. Eventually, I lift a piece of paper. As it rises almost to my chest, I give out, and the paper floats toward the crowd. They cheer wildly and throw bills and coins in my direction. I place my fingers around a quarter and act as if I'm going to pocket it, but it's no use; it's too heavy, and it drops, which causes them to pitch even more money at me, knowing that I don't have the strength to spend it. When I pretend to faint, dropping into my cot, my lover signals for the crowd to empty out. When they leave, she collects the money and counts it before locking it away in a trunk. "You outdid yourself, honey," she says, even if I didn't. When we make love, it's from a distance. She blows kisses at me with her hand. I catch them with my lips and close my eyes.

Thanksgiving for a Diner Clown

When you notice a clown at a diner on Thanksgiving, it means there's nobody interested in the exhibit of his life. And here is one of those dreadful holidays when the bone inside a clown's head heats up, and he conjures his girl's sweet breath; the flesh that covers his heart can still dream. She's been gone for years, and yet he's hardly breathing, staring at the door of the diner as if she's only just parking her car. He was always neglecting the real act while juggling birds. Time doesn't heal him. It breaks him down until he can smell her perfume in the cranberry sauce. It wears him away like rain on concrete.

Nightshade

I was only as tall as her calla lilies but my arms were acrobatic. I could do handstands, walk up a staircase upside down. I could dance like a wounded angel. My arms were like tubers, stronger than my mother's legs.

Growing up, I had one friend my age, but Mom claimed he was a profiteer. He had read about me in the newspaper, he said. He brought me M&Ms and we played with my Mr. Potato kit. Once he kissed me and I leaped toward his face. I kissed him back so hard his lips were bloody, and he gasped for breath, his face turning all rooty. "This can only end badly," mother said and kicked him out.

When I complained about being lonely, she said anyone who came over had a plot to steal me. "You have stalks for legs. You know how much you'd be worth on the black market?" What black market?" I'd ask. "Don't argue with me. I know what I'm talking about," she'd say. But no one else came over.

* * *

On my sixteenth birthday I pumped her for answers about why she really wanted to keep me hidden. "You can't imagine how toxic you are," she said. "There isn't an alkalinizing recipe that can diffuse you."

Across the border there was a store that sold cheap fur jackets. Mother asked me what color I wanted. I wanted the brown. I'd seen them in photographs, it looked like walnut tree bark. She brought home a grey. The dark grey fur made me look like an eggplant.

* * *

More and more often, I tricked my mother. I would hide

under my bed with my window wide open, wind and rain streaming in and pooling on my rug, hoping to make her think that I'd jumped down into our garden. I'd hear her walk in, gasp, and then go into hysterics. I'd crawl out to her, a bundle of dangerous dreams. "I'm changing," I'd say, my stalks just beginning to sprout.

Eddie at Home

We knew he'd eventually have to join the circus. He was always trying to fill his stomach, but it was getting impossible. His size twenty-five shoes thumping the kitchen floor, mother urging him not to deny himself, because he was a growing boy. "You're halfway to heaven," she'd say. "Ma, it's impossible," would echo through the house. I'd be in my bedroom, working on my dance moves, wondering what would become of my brother, eight feet tall; who would pick all three of us up and carry us around in the crook of his arm. We tried to console him, but he was outgrowing his human heart. "You're not strange to us," we said, "but you'll be a stranger to everyone else." It was always raining when Eddie got sad, tears flooding down his face.

Mom was so worried on our last night with Eddie, cooking up noodles in the kitchen. Dad saying, "Eddie, lad, you know where to find us; please take care of yourself." My brother, our beautiful giant, on his last day in our house, offered me up his oarlike-pinkie finger, led me out into the living room to dance to the music I loved and said I would be a star one day. His head scraped the ceiling as we danced. Our house wanted simply to be big enough for him.

My Circus Grandmother

Grandma's air had been sucked out of her days. A few decades retired, the tattoos on her body drooped as if they were looking for water. Her bright purple flowers faded into a mauve cloud. Her dragons looked more like stuffed pets. Her snake swallowed her waist.

Once she told me she missed the drunken card game afternoons. Missed the rude duck sounds of the clowns. She was angry as a bulldog until her afternoon wine.

I was twelve and still felt like a picture on the wall, as if waiting for my life to become a life. The heat of summer days buzzing over my skin. I'd make myself a dry turkey sandwich, flipping through childhood.

"I know what I want," I told her, "I want to be an illustrated lady like you," I said.

She nodded excitedly as if I just got the right answer to the million-dollar question.

"Monkeyface," she told me the year she contracted cancer, "I was broken all my life, but it never made me any less interesting." There was a lump in her gut, and it wouldn't stop growing.

I held her hand, curled up like a hawk's talon. I told her jokes that I heard on TV.

She laughed. "You're no stand up comic, but Grandma loves you darling, hallelujah."

* * *

She had a tattoo of a clown on each of her biceps. I loved those clowns, those arms. In the end, the clowns seemed to fall asleep where her muscles used to be. When I cradled her head, her last laugh broke on my cheek.

The Former Bearded Lady in the Circus

When the bearded lady woke up, her face was pressed into the pillow—nothing between her skin and the rough dirty pillowcase. She noticed some loose fluff on her hand after touching her chin. Her beard was gone. She felt it repeatedly to be sure. She had been a little girl the last time her face was smooth. She wasn't sad that it was gone, but how would she keep her job? And what had moved her to get rid of it? She remembered splitting last night's cheap bottle of bourbon with the lobster man, how he had seduced her and gently spread the soapy foam on her face. The foam felt good, cool to the touch—how with a straight razor, he had shaved her clean, her face opening in the mirror like an exotic blossom under clear water, petals peeling away until her face was the water. How he held her and said, "Bearded no more, but still beautiful." He carried the hair away in a bucket, tossing it into the air. And how they had danced under the light of the dust-colored moon, and no one recognized her, not even the circus manager, while lobster man caressed her up and down with a dozen prickly arms.

The Saddest Woman on Earth

She claimed to be "the saddest woman on earth." I emailed her to say, "That'll change when you meet me. I'll bring a smile to your face." When she came to the door, she had a sad long face with a wide frown as if she had just received tragic news. "Everything okay," I asked. "No," she said, "Nothing's okay, but I have to move forward." Her home seemed very sad with its gray walls and dim lighting. There were few decorations, only a vase with wilted yellow flowers. Her small dog, possibly a terrier mix, didn't even get up to sniff me. "What kind of dog," I asked. "I don't know," she said. "I found him in the park one day and took him home." I was planning to take her out, but she had cooked dinner, unsalted roast chicken, boiled potatoes and greens without dressing. I cut into the chicken, and it was undercooked and cold. "I'm not a good cook," she said. I disposed of the meal, cleaned off the plates, and put them in the dishwasher. Then I ordered Chinese food: General Tso's chicken, spring rolls, beef and broccoli. The smells were delicious, and who can resist General Tso? She ate two helpings and so did I, and the dog perked up when I offered him some beef. Then he leaned against my knee. She and her dog appeared to be smiling. I had already come through on my promise. Later, the saddest woman and I made love several times. She closed her eyes and moaned with pleasure. Then we lay under the covers together. Her dog jumped in bed with us. Before I left in the morning, I kissed her on the forehead. "Smile, I said. She shook her head and looked down at the ground. "This," "she said, "just makes me sadder."

Goldfish Skin

I won the goldfish in the hoop-toss booth. Mom brought me to the carnival, and first-off we bought some ice cream, but it melted all over my dress. I cried. Mom shook her head and said there was nothing wrong with a little spillage, but she didn't think we should buy anymore treats. "Try to win something instead," she said.

I had five dollars to spend on games, had saved it up with my allowance, for babysitting myself when Mom had to go to the store because sometimes she didn't come back until morning. After the car crash killed my father, she was not as interested in cooking and would often be hunting for takeout, sometimes be gone for hours. For babysitting myself, she gave me money and told me that for my birthday we'd go to the carnival.

At the Ring-the-Duck booth, there was a drum-roll soundtrack. "Ready, one two three," the man said. I tossed the hoop over a floating plastic duck's head. "Tada!" A gong gonged. That's hard to achieve, young lady, the man said, throwing a shark grin at Mom. Mom's lips straightened, and her eyes watered with pride.

The man had a fatherly chin and block-shaped yellow teeth. I won, but I knew, the minute he handed me the goldfish in a baggie, that a silly little fish couldn't survive like this. The timer was ticking. Since the accident, I wanted to know about the bad things that were going to happen before they actually happened. Part of us was missing and would never grow back, and it was going to be a hard game to win.

Mom put me in charge. Her manual dexterity had been

changed by the accident, and she had a hard time knowing what time of day it was and which meal we were supposed to be eating. That year there was a drought, and we sat on the front porch together and talked about how beautiful the golden clouds were. "That color," Mom said, "reminds me of goldfish skin."

Kissing Booth

"Kiss kiss," my customers shout as they wait, as the pigeons waddle around them and the stray dogs gather into a pack at the bandstand. The farm stalls, the cheese booths, the food carts have small lines but mine extends the length of the green. The price is steep, but kisses aren't easy to come by in these times, and my lips are soft, moist—capable. I kiss the ones that need tenderness with extra care. Those who require tough love, I kiss hard forcing my lips down on theirs. And those who look ready to faint, I oxygenate with long breathy kisses that expand their chests and straighten their spine. And for a large tip, I let the rich well-dressed ones feel the silk of my tongue. My customers don't seem to care that they could be kissing my disease. For that matter, I could be kissing theirs. When my pucker begins losing its grip, that means I'm running out of kisses like a cellphone battery down to the last 10%. "Last three kisses," I say, holding up three fingers. I sustain each one as long as I can, and the customer tries to hold me even longer, but I'm adept at getting away. When I shut the curtain, the crowd applauds and shouts, "More! More!" I stick my hand out and wave good-bye.

Almost Anything

I swallow a sword, a scimitar to be precise, but she shakes her head. "It's just another trick," she says. "You're good at them." She has temporomandibular disorder and rubs her jaw when she watches me open my mouth wide enough to eat a small rabbit. "It's not a trick," I say, "it's a death-defying feat that only a few can accomplish." "Not necessary," she says, massaging her cheekbones. "Want to make a bet on what I can do," I say, and I light the kindling in our fireplace by blowing yellow flames into the air. When the fire is gone, I exhale smoke and ash. My lips singed, I hurry to the sink and run cold water over them and into my mouth. She touches my arm. "Are you hurt?" I nod and shut off the faucet. "That doesn't happen normally. I must have swallowed too much hot air." I consider swallowing something simple such as a toaster oven or a set of plates to demonstrate that I'm still a master—even though I occasionally wound myself. She opens her hand, and a small tube of aloe lip balm appears. "Try some," she says, "it'll take the sizzle out."

Some Girls Swallow the Concept of Hell

Pearl tells us that she remembers how, as a child, it was hard to sit on her father's lap because his belly poured over his trousers and it looked a bit uncomfortable and it poked her in the back like a spike. "Oh fuck," we say, one of us straight-faced and the other giggling, but she's not joking and seems preoccupied. Her eyes are drippy and sad like she's going over it in her head. "And he'd tell me how funny I was, holding me there like a bat."

Pearl says she's happy to live in hell since her father pre-booked her into heaven. We too are happy to live here in hell. We hope to remain here in hell for the rest of our lives.

* * *

We agree that Pearl's funny. We also agree about how it's been terrible watching her pace like a lovesick raccoon outside of Large Eddie's caravan before he lets her in. Eddie, whose most famous trick is to break an iron chain over his heart by pushing out his rib cage. Sometimes we watch Pearl and Eddie through his window, the way he tries to mount her makes us squeamish, and this reminds us both of something we don't know what to do about.

"Sweet little mousie mousie," Eddies grunts, because Pearl's sword-swallowing and glass walking skills don't impress him as much as this.

* * *

Today Pearl seems clear that no good will come from loving a man who can carry a horse on his shoulders and laugh. She serves us two glasses of plum wine and chocolate bit cookies, and we slide onto one chair and listen. She has never choked on a sword or a fire manipulation act or a circus strong man, she tells us, holding a wet little hanky. She's writing a letter for us to deliver to Eddie and she seals it with candle wax and isn't sure which one of us to hand it to.

I take it from her and slide it into our velvet handbag, which is slung over my sister's shoulders.

"Be dust, you two. I have to perform, and I need to fix up my disgusting face."

* * *

The clown wishes Pearl luck and warms the audience up by serenading Pearl with "The Way You Do the Things You Do." The audience laughs at his act, him swinging his hips and batting his five-inch eyelashes like dusters. Pearl stands ready in her satin dress, beaming at the audience, holding the sword against her thigh. "Through my lips, lookout tongue, excuse me stomach, here it comes!"

The promise always seems to calm her down. She lays the sword flat against the back of her throat and plunges. We hold in our guts. Pearl stares up at the lights as if she's digesting her Eddie. She holds him down inside her body so long it's as if we can all finally breathe.

Return of the Dead Magician

When I downloaded the circus App, my late husband, a magician, popped up again. He'd popped up often since the time of his failure, this time taking residence inside my cracked phone. Inside the distorted glass, his extended smile floated like seaweed. He was still wearing his hat and moustache, but his cape now looked flimsy. He'd died while being imprisoned in a cage underwater with a huge padlock. I thought about deleting the App, but decided to see what he could pull off this time around.

Within seconds, he picked the lock. Removing his cuffs, he carved a seam in the glass and escaped another death, sliding into my living room. "That's some trick," I said. "Now please make yourself disappear again." "I can't. The App doesn't work that way," he said, soaked to the bone and dripping rainbow puddles on the rug.

The Angel Act

Every night the crowd poured into his tent to watch him open his graying wings, to see him blow blessings at the multitudes, to see him levitate to the top of the big tent without a rope. One night a young girl asked if the angel would touch her little head with a pointed feather. "I made a wish for you!" cried the girl, and he felt the wind blowing against him cease so that he could fly unimpeded. "There's something fishy about this angel," said the kid's mother, blowing her horse lips into the air. "My daughter trusts a freak with wings, but she doesn't even let me read to her anymore." The crowd laughed, but it wasn't funny. The angel rose higher above them, a nimbus of light around his head.

The angel had discovered he was an angel when he was a young boy. The moment his drunk father slapped his mother, the boy opened his wings, floating through the living room. "Get down," the father shouted, so the angel touched him on the shoulder, and his father let go of his anger. "I'm sick," the father said and lay down on the couch.

Now the angel looked down at the girl and the faces of the men and women so full of doubt and desire, wanting to believe. He could levitate inside the tent, but not relieve their pain. They cheered and threw money, and a few of the older ones fell asleep. When they were finally gone, the angel collected the fallen bills and coins and walked over to the fairgrounds for a hot dog.

The Quiet Woman

She was so quiet she had blended with the shadows. "Shh!" The crowds whispered, waiting for her to enter the tent. "Is she in here yet?" A loudmouth in a Hawaiian shirt blurted. She held up her arm and waved. The quiet woman began speaking, her lips moving vigorously as if she were chewing steak. "Huh?" the impatient crowd buzzed. "Is she eating air?" "I think I hear some words," another woman shrieked, and someone else bellowed, "a pink butterfly leaped from her lips!" An argumentative woman Boo-d, shouting for her money back while others began to grow faint. Now the quiet woman could see something fluttering toward her from the back of the tent, something shapeless and mistlike, a vapor floating toward her over the crowd. She opened her mouth and pointed to the back of her throat; the crowd went silent with anticipation. She caught the pink vapor with her hands and swallowed it whole, taking it deep into her lungs and letting out a staccato of syllables that was so loud the people in the front row could almost hear it.

Last Bow of the Clown

No one talked to him. No one visited him in his tent and watched him put on his clown suit. No one saw him paint his face white with big thick red lips. No one even knew where his tent was. The ringmaster didn't introduce him to the crowd, celebrating his accomplishments and asking for a big round of applause. No other performer came to see his act. No one even paid him to perform, but still he showed up day and night and did his tricks, honking his nose and waving his big floppy shoes, tripping and falling, bumping his head against the railing. No one in the crowd laughed, or clapped, or threw money into the ring. And no one remained in their seats when the clown took his final bow.

Section 3

Motown and More

Memories of Motown

It makes me sad to think about how my father, the magician, loved to dance with me, how he'd turn me in the living room to "Love Is Here Standing By" or "My Girl." I'd stare up at him like he was my Houdini, and he'd lead me right into his own haze of smoke, a cigarette dangling from his lips. He danced with me instead of my sister, danced with me instead of my mom, a slippery grin on his face, oblivious to anything but moving with me to the music. My sister cried until my mom held her, swaying together in the living room, slow dancing to "Smoke Gets in Your Eyes" as my father folded me so far into himself that for the rest of my childhood, I disappeared.

Looking for Motown

He stops on every corner and looks up at the signs and buildings with a big smile on his face as if he recognizes it all. "We're in Motown," he says. "How do you know?" I ask, not wanting to disappoint him. He puts his hand behind his ear, trying to catch the sound emerging from the street. "Listen," he says, "the sidewalks, the streets, the buildings are singing 'The Way You Do the Things You Do.'" I'm not sure why they'd be singing that song over "Heat Wave" or "Baby Love," but I nod anyway, even though I can't hear anything but noise and traffic. He pulls me forward, and we're running from block to block. "It's all Motown," he says. "Isn't Motown in Detroit?" I ask. "You don't understand Motown," he says and takes out his harmonica and begins playing a broken version of "Fingertips" on a street corner, with a sign that says "Whistle." People passing by chuckle or smile—some snort—and a few toss coins at his feet. I smile at him and pretend to be grooving to the music, swaying my hips and moving my shoulders rhythmically. *Is this what it means to be in love*, I wonder. He wipes off his harmonica and sheathes it in his pocket. "Motown," he says, "It's just the beginning," but for me it's the end.

Along Comes Mary

like a sweet smell in the air, a pink vapor. Along comes Mary with her bushel of hair and her eyes that have ransacked your cities before. She knocks on your door, and your door is gone. She enters your house, and there is no house. Along comes Mary, slipping off your mask, kissing you so hard, your lips bruise, slipping her tongue into your mouth until you are breathing only her breath. With her silky hand, she touches you so gently, it's like a punch in the gut. With her breathy voice, she lights your candles and puts them out. Along comes Mary like a wind swirling the debris, like the sun shining through your ruins, like the sky enclosing you in its blue wings.

What Is It About Mary

When I say Mary came along, I opened the door because she was knocking softly. I had never seen her before. She said, "I'm Mary." "Hey Mary, nice to meet you and… are you okay?" I said so unused to seeing humans in the flesh.

The voice felt unpracticed. When necessary, I talked to humans on my phone or on my computer, but I hadn't felt lonely until I saw Mary. Nobody had seen me in the flesh in years and one day Mary appears knocking lightly on my door—wearing a hedgehog mask. Stranger in hedgehog mask beckoning!

So, I followed Mary outside my house. The air felt fantastic. And there she was, a woman who seemed as peaceful as a hedgehog. I followed Mary outside like a feeling.

The night before, she explained, she had planted her husband in the backyard. When we got to Mary's house she took me right back there and he was sniffling alone in the gloaming. This was his and Mary's yard, filled with neglected looking fruit trees.

"Here's a friend for you, Bill," Mary said. He was sitting there in an unfashionable mask all tied up, and she left us there together. "Be back in a bit," Mary said.

I asked him about Mary. "What is it about your wife?" I said. "Along she came," he smiled, his lips fanning out in confirmation. I had never recognized how much I needed to be set free until Mary came along, I told him.

Mary came out, still in her mask, and asked us if we wanted some herbal tea. We both said, "Yes Mary!" It was as if we'd always wanted a hedgehog to make us a cup of herbal tea in the middle of a stinky yard.

Broken Man

He and I meet in a cheap hotel room. Broken lamp, broken springs, broken shower. He cocks an eyebrow at me because I've broken my New Year's Resolution. He's touching my bad knee, saying he likes my rickety gait. When we make love, the shrunken fitted sheet pops off the disabled mattress. "Figures," I say, but the joke breaks in half. My telephone is ringing like a drunken mother's argument. He is disapproving of the call, does not believe in phone calls or mothers. "Never needed no mother in prison," he tells me. I feel sorry for him and all of his interrupted stories. He looks at me as if he's wearing a choke-collar. "Choke collars never teach a dog anything," I tell myself.

Picking Up the Moose

At a party, I met a moose who was dating a bear. A drink in his paw, the bear was in the corner with a pretty cat with bright violet eyes. *What's with these animals?* I wondered. The bear looked a little sleazy. But the moose was really very attractive with big eyes and a prominent nose. She was wearing some kind of strong perfume that attracted and repulsed me. "It looks as though your bear has found a cat," I said. She snorted. I took that as a sign she agreed. "What do you say we go home together?" I asked. "I don't date dogs," she said. "That seems a little inflexible," I replied. She kicked the ground several times with her hooves. Does that mean she wants to dance? Or is that dancing for a moose? "My Girl" was playing, and all the other animals were slow dancing. When she pulled away from me, I barked several times. That got me a lot of nasty looks, but not from the moose, who faced me again. "Forget the bear," I said. I took off my mask. "I'm not a dog," I said. "Well, what are you then?" she said. She took off her mask, and she was still a moose. I saw the bear outside the window chasing the cat up a tree. The moose began shifting her weight back and forth on her long legs, and pretty soon we were dancing cheek to cheek.

Where Motown Lives

When the tour busses dry up, and a few older couples wander through Detroit staring at abandoned buildings, a man says, "I wonder why they called it that. Where is the mo? Where is the town?" Another man starts googling instead of singing. "But my Dad loved Motown," a woman says, tears slipping down her face. Her husband tries to calm her, you can see his feet moving to the beat of some distant drum. Who can show them how it lives inside the sounds of the cars rushing by, the long drip of love from a bird's solemn flight?

Broken Man, Broken Woman

She and I meet at the main corner of a broken town. Since the wheels of her suitcase are broken, I offer to carry it for her, but she refuses. We enter the broken hotel and pay the man at the desk, his face wide with cracks. "There are numbers," he says. "You'll find it," but he knows we know the way. Her cellphone keeps twittering, but she lets it go. We enter a broken room and turn on the lights—still so dim I can barely make out the features of her face. "We really should meet somewhere else," she says, but whenever I ask where we should meet, she always chooses this place. "I promised myself I wouldn't come here again," she says. In the shadows, she picks up her phone, signaling me with her hand that I should not say anything. When it's over, she tells me that she had to answer. Her mother is ill. "We should stop this," she says, "before it's too late." "It's already too late," I answer, "We should just try a different hotel, one with a bed that has clean sheets that don't slip off every two seconds."

Cramped Love

When we make love, the springs pop, the plaster falls, and as she mounts me, I can see the crack running the length of the ceiling with its water stains. At first, she holds it all in; her eyes grow wide as if she has seen an eagle hovering behind me, ready to pluck me from her body. Then she lets out a cry, knocking me with such force, I fly backwards off the bed. She shakes her leg and holds it straight, slowly raising it up and down with her hips. "Did you come?" I ask, proud of myself for eliciting such an orgasm. "No," she says, "I had a terrible cramp in my leg. It was like a wheel turning over inside it." She moves her knee up and down and then lengthens her leg. "I think it's okay now," she says. I get back in bed and begin to kiss her again, but she stops me. "Let's just lie here together." Since I don't really have a choice, I agree. After a while she tells me stories about the sadness of her sisters. I tell her about the many problems of my non-existent brother.

The Death of Motown

The town tries to remember hearing about the death of itself through the grapevine. It tries to remember how it used to feel like someone's girl. But when it looks down, it is standing in front of a new producer's mansion, ringing the doorbell. The world keeps dancing, but no one comes to the door.

Walking Away from Motown

"You were already ruined when I met you," you said. As always, you called me by the name you gave me: "Renee." Which wasn't my name. According to you, we were in Motown, and songs poured out of the windows like rain. I looked down at my legs, and they wouldn't move, as if stuck to the glittery pavement. "Just walk away, Renee" you said, "and see how far you get." I couldn't move. "You think I'm someone in a Four Tops Song," I answered, "but really the Left Banke wrote that song, and they had nothing to do with Motown." "Who remembers the Left Banke?" you said. "The Four Tops made the song famous." Wind swept debris down the street. I brushed my hair out of my eyes. "You're the one always walking away," I said, trying to remember one good day we had together. "And my real name is Jesse." Before you walked away, you said, "No one ever wrote a song about Jesse," but you got that wrong also.

Section 4

Messing with Love

What You Can't Fix

She was always fixing me, stuffing filler in my holes, applying putty or crazy glue to seal off any cracks to be sure nothing got in. She would pace in front of me as if I were a sculpture, looking at me and thinking and then she would release herself, satisfied for the moment that the holes were gone and that I was becoming something beautiful and solid. Still there were holes in my mind she couldn't fix, holes where the light got in and sometimes snow and rain, holes where my thoughts escaped when they had to. But when she put on her blue satin kimono and hovered near me, I could forgive her. When we made love, it was like hearing the rain beat on the roof, knowing it will not get in.

Out of Touch

He touched the window, and the window dissolved. A hummingbird hovered, staring into his eyes, then flew away. A bee bounced off his cheek, and a fly circled his head. He caught it, but when he opened his hand, the fly was gone. He picked up a glass of water from the counter, and the glass vanished, the water spilling out. He touched the water, and the counter was no longer wet. When his lover came into the kitchen, he was staring at a hole where the faucet used to be. "What did you do to the faucet?" she asked. "I touched it," he said, "Everything I touch disappears." To demonstrate, he touched a mug she had given him on his birthday, featuring their smiling faces. It vanished. His lover looked at him—unimpressed. "You're the opposite of a superhero," she said. "I didn't know there was such a thing," he said. He touched her hair, and a clump of it fell out in his hand. "Give that back!" she said. He handed the clump back to her, and she stuck it in her pocket. "Will you make me disappear?" she said. She was married and they had been seeing each other secretly for years. "Are you kidding?" he said. When they lay down on the bed together, he told her he would never let her disappear. He let his hand pass over her body without touching it. "That feels good," she said, her eyes closing. "Do it again." This time his fingertips almost grazed her breasts, and she shivered as if touched by a feather. "Again," she said as if speaking to him in a dream or trance. Too close for comfort, he thought and lifted his hand, still moving it over her body. Outside the window, there were no bird sounds at all. There were the sounds of a quiet storm starting up, branches beating against the hole where the window used to be.

Flying Off

Angry, my lover left that night dressed in colorful plumage—wings outspread. I shouted, "You always fly off when we're getting to the bottom of things." Later I lit a candle and turned off the lights, but she didn't come back. In the morning I found a single orange feather.

Fish Story

"I'm blue," she says to her goldfish, remembering the canopy of her married lover's heavy-lidded eyes, unnervingly bright in the darkness. She and her married lover had purchased a family of goldfish and the aquarium together at the local pet shop. The owner warned them not to overfeed the fish or they'd get tail rot and die. Of course, they overfed the fish, and only this one survived, with his lonely gold glow. Now, the fish reminds her of how he abandoned her. "I can't keep doing this to you," he said. And she answered, "Yes, you can." They went around like this in circles, and it was obvious what he meant. Christmases she celebrated alone with the fish, and he felt guilty. He'd taken home his toiletry kit with his musk cologne that smelled like something had died, his electric shaver, his aqua blue toothpaste, the balm to prevent his thighs from chafing. He was getting paunchy, and sometimes during sex, his body had seemed to float around on top of her. When he fell off her, she chuckled to think of him belly-up. As she stares at the goldfish, the goldfish presses up at the glass staring back at her. *Where do goldfish meander in the wild?* she wonders and *how do they survive?* Is there really such a thing as a wild goldfish? She's hardly been able to look at the fish since her lover left. "It's you and me against the world, kid," she says as the goldfish puckers its lips against glass.

Moose Stand Off

When my boyfriend announces he's leaving me for a moose, at first I'm hurt. How can you feel attracted to a moose? "She's not as anxious as you," he says. "She doesn't have to pee every half hour, and she's not always mad at me for smoking pot." A parrot flies over my boyfriend's building, screaming. A car alarm bellows like a difficult animal. "I think we're making each other worse." He has a point. I can never imagine our future together, both of us flighty, unable to hold on to a job, overly anxious. So, I get into my car, put on my headphones, and listen to Saint-Saëns "Carnival of the Animals." I think, maybe it's time to learn the glass harmonica.

An hour later I go back over to his apartment wearing some Halloween moose antlers. "Elkish!" he says, letting me in, admiring my horns from the back. "Nope. Moosish…" I say. Then, from his bedroom, comes a long, drawn out moan like an oboe and the moose saunters in, ready to charge. So I spray the air between us with Bach Flower Remedy and give a little harmless shrug. "I'm tired of conflict!" my boyfriend says. Then he lights up a joint

Refusing a smoke, the moose and I saunter into his backyard. Pot makes us paranoid. I shake out my frizzy mop. "Your hair, in the moonlight," the moose's eyes seem to say, "looks wild. It's a mess." I giggle, turning on my smile, feeling *seen*, feeling deeply *female*. We walk back into the apartment, arm in arm.

My boyfriend removes his mask and he's an old stoner who resembles my father. I whip off my antlers, and I'm just like my mother, a woman who has never been good at relationships. The moose whips off her mask. "I was never actually a moose," she says. She and I get into my car where we listen to Carnival of the Animals and snuggle calmy, imagining our songs on the glass harmonica.

The Charm of the Foul-Mouthed Wife

Friends were supportive of Ralph's remarriage, but they didn't understand the new wife's cursing, or the hold she had on Ralph. They'd arrive at a dinner party and his wife would say, "What a fucking great view! Would you look at this wild-assed lamp? How about that goddamn traffic! That's why it took us so fucking long!"

Friends would ski off to the kitchen. The host would lean into a shot of whiskey. "She was expelled from the Brownies when she was only ten years old," Ralph explained. His previous wife was so polite. Now it was like he'd walked in with a foul-mouthed African parrot and nobody knew what to say.

"You really got a hold on me, baby," would play in Ralph's mind. The new wife may not know how to enter a party but if there were ants in their kitchen she knew how to kill them. She'd murder one ant at a time, with nail polish remover. "Entomologically speaking, each of these fuckers is the same as the bastard right behind it."

At night she'd squint at him from the dark of their bedroom cave. "It's cold as a witch's tit," she'd say. Under the covers, he'd warm up her toes and beg her to do her entire repertoire. She'd begin with asshole and end with a wank. After that, she'd fall asleep. Too excited to breathe, he'd go outside and lay down on a lawn chair—just marveling at his luck, watching stars pop like spittle.

Hall of Masks

I removed the mask to kiss her, but there was another mask. I removed that too, and there was still another mask. "Aren't some of those masks unnecessary?" I asked. "There are masks that require disguises," she said. "I only want to kiss you," I answered. "Spittle, banana breath, lip friction—who kisses anymore?" Instead, I brushed her mask with my mask—a mask kiss. She rolled her eyes. Then I slipped my hand inside her tights and felt something vaguely familiar. I removed her tights, but she was wearing another pair of tights. I removed them also, only to find another pair of tights. "Is it healthy to wear that many layers?" I asked. "I'm not bothered," she said, "I just put them on until I feel less naked." I slipped my fingers inside yet another pair of tights. "Are you searching for something?" she asked. "I hadn't thought about it," I said and then she removed me.

The End of her Blue Period

When she picks up the blue man from a dance rehearsal, she invites him to stay and offers him supper. "I'll pop over to Safeway for red," he says. When he returns, he's holding a bottle of wine without a label and some blue irises that have probably been stolen from someone's garden. "Here, you take these," he says, "and I'll put on some music," and it's just at that moment, she realizes that his blue eyes are not really blue, and his wan face reminds her of cold oatmeal. Still, the room brightens from his irises. She lives in a gray apartment building sandwiched between two smelly parking lots. She painted her walls off-white, but the off-white has turned grayish with the smoke and fumes coming in the windows from the parking lots. She would keep them shut, but her stuffy apartment needs air to circulate. As always, in the evening after dinner, the blue man streams the blues, closing his eyes and singing the words to "You Put a Spell on Me." But now she's no longer sure what's going to come next. "I might even love you," she whispers to the blue man while he sleeps, his hair nesting in the hollow of her rose-colored pillowcase. She says it to the back of his unconscious head, lips dangerously close to his ear, "You're part of my blue period." And then, it's not a dream anymore. One day she wakes up and finds her feelings can be painted blue. When she tells him goodbye, she memorizes the pinkness of his skin under the blue.

Heading toward Vegas

After the motorcycle wreck, her muscles became loose. She felt as if her skin might fall off her bones. She rose and sat back down twenty times each day, and yet the strength in her legs seemed to be waning. She played ambient-celestial music, because she liked the gentle way it tinkled out and helped her to imagine herself floating through the rooms of her small house. She strung fairy lights on her walker, so in the dark she would always bring light. She used her cellphone camera to photograph her leather jacket, captioned it, "Born to ride again," and posted it on Facebook, where she received hundreds of hearts and 350 likes with best wishes and photos of motorcycle riders in the golden sun. Her cat jumped up on her knees, scratching at her jeans until it settled on her lap. She was content for a while, purring along with her cat and eventually, she would close her eyes and sink into a nap. The cat would wake her, leaping off her lap. The sun came in the window, and the shadows fell across the wood floor. She rose and sat, rose and sat, until she was tired once again, and sweat welled up in her eyes. She was breathing heavily, and she could almost feel the blood in her legs. She was getting better—she was sure, but words and faces kept falling through the hole in her mind, and she couldn't even remember Freddie's face, only the hump of his back on that morning when she locked her arms around his waist, as he gunned his motorcycle toward Vegas, the flaming lights over the desert dying in her eyes.

Betrayal

When I returned after one night away, my lover had let another lover move in and changed the lock on the door. Inside, I could hear them talking and laughing. "Honey, when can I see you?" I shouted. "Get lost," she shrieked, laughing and hooting it up with her new lover. "What about my things?" I asked. "What things?" She yelled through the keyhole. "Everything is mine." I shouted and banged on the door until the door cracked. She opened the door on the chain. "Go away!" she said and handed me a folded piece of paper, with a list of payments I owed her, including the estimated price of a new door.

Dusk

Today, he sees me because today, it pleases him to see me and because today, he wants more than anything to see himself the way I see him. "You are who you are," I respond, unwilling to reveal anything more. Today, he holds nothing in his hands as if it were a bouquet of flowers. And as he follows me through my cottage, I walk past the bedroom, out the back door into the garden, where now the air is thick with bugs, and dusk has fallen.

Birds Don't Like You

"You have a bad relationship with birds," Adelia says as we walk down the road, not talking about our real problem. "That's absolute nonsense," I reply. But when the mourning doves see me, they go silent, and starlings rain down globs of white shit onto my hat. "I love birds," I say, "even if they don't believe it." Swooping through the sky, a hawk plunges directly at my head. "You see?" she says and backs away. The hawk snags me by the hair with its talons, ready to carry me off to her nest. "Well, at least someone wants me," I shout trying to shake myself free at first, and then giving in. In seconds we're high above the ground, flying like predatory angels, staring down at Adelia who resembles a red bug from so high above. She is looking straight up at the sky, her tiny lips moving, probably whispering "I told you so…" as I ride into a swirl of cloud, dangling like an old skin about to be shed.

Snow Wonder

On our fortieth anniversary, we returned to the same ski resort where we had our honeymoon in the 1990s. The original resort was long gone, but there was a new one that guaranteed snow. "You could never count on it before," you said, as if the world had finally become more reasonable. "But it was the real thing," I said. "powdery and beautiful. That's got to count for something." "The important thing is skiing," you said, "not praying for snow." I agreed, remembering our disappointment when there wasn't enough snow or the snow was slushy. But it was all good back then. The sun glared in the window, but you squinted and looked out at the slopes. "This resort has the most expensive artificial snow on the planet," you said. "They do this kind of special misting with water from a giant spray bottle." "Do you remember touching the real stuff?" I asked. "Not really. And the artificial is so much better," you said, kissing me on my new lips. "You're perfect," you said. "And so are you," I said, kissing you on a sixty-year-old face without wrinkles, clean and pure as artificial snow.

Quiet

Quiet touches your shoulder as you enter your living room. Rolls up to you like a wave that is so soft it barely moves or a fly that floats through the hallway half dead. It grazes your lips, settles in your tea. You swallow it down, holding Quiet in your larynx for as long as you can take it. Later, it wakes you in the middle of the morning, tapping you on the shoulder. "I'm cheap," it says, reminding you of all of the broken lovers it will protect you from. "You'll never have to say I'm sorry because you'll never offend," it says. Quiet reminds you of your mother's face washed by blue TV light, the look of despair while she watched the news. It reminds you of the lover you never recognized, the one who might have really loved you.

Mime Love

When I was young, I fell in love with a mime, who loved me back, but never actually touched me. She would deliver her love from a distance, moving her body sinuously as if she had no bones. Sometimes she would draw pictures of her love for me on a window that didn't exist. She kissed the air and pointed at me. She tapped her heart with her hand and seemed to melt. She would reach out and mime tugging a rope to pull me toward her. But if I would actually walk toward her, she backed into a shadow and remained so still I wasn't even sure she was in the room. "Why don't we ever make love?" I asked. "We do make love," she answered, speaking with her hands. Once, I watched her pantomime our lovemaking, playing both parts, herself and me. She was so good I could feel a shiver run through my body, so good I was almost happy.

Pet Loss

Since Hubert the Bearded Dragon died, the thing that cheered me up was having sex with my diner customers. The first one was Taylor, middle-aged, married and polyamorous, hugged like a boa constrictor. "Pet loss is so hard," he'd say, squeezing me like a pinkie mouse, making me feel like I was alive again. After one of our love-making sessions he ended up in the hospital with heart failure. I visited him there, thinking that Hubert would have liked the unnatural warmth of the hospital room.

His wife Alexis was by his bedside. "I usually see you in your diner outfit," she said. She gave me a lift home in her Honda. "He'll be fine," she said, thinking that I was worried about her husband. I invited her into my apartment. "That was Hubert's terrarium," I said, pointing to a cluttered corner of the room. I still had his U.V. light plugged in. She stared at the pet loss support group fliers, hugged me as hard as her husband did. "Losing a pet is like losing a dream," she said, moving in to kiss me.

After Taylor and Alexis, there was Charlene, who owned the Critter Center, and wanted to harvest my eggs. I could imagine my babies hatching in an incubator, but not in another woman's belly. "You and I would make beautiful creatures," she said at the end of my shift, kissing me with the most beautiful scaly lips.

Then it was Fernando, a retired bullfighter with scars all over his body. I asked him if he'd like to meet me after work, to accompany me to the Critter Center and help me chose one of the baby iguanas. "That one looks a little bit like you," he said, pointing to a wise looking buggy-eyed lizard. Afterward, making love with me on my Alligator patterned rug, he promised me his couch in Spain whenever I wanted to travel. "I've never been to Spain," I said, "can I bring the iguana?" He said, "why not?" and left me with a case of herpes and the promise of a climate so warm that a reptile wouldn't need a UV bulb to stay alive.

Then there was Ilya, who sat at the counter and waited for me to arrive each day. "I take you home," he would say and "make you happy." In the corner of his apartment, he had an aquarium with only one fish. "Where are the other fish?" I asked. "I had a piranha," he said, "he ate all the others." I stared at the fish, who looked lonely and useless, like a castaway who has lost the will to float.

Ilya removed my jacket and kissed me sweetly on the lips, "I can be your prince," he said, his big Russian eyes full of soulfulness. "Be my frog instead," I said. He squatted down on all fours and croaked.

Section 5

Curse of the Family

Owl Eyes

Her father rescued the owl, nearly dead, tail feathers mutilated. He lived permanently in her backyard in a homemade cage, so tame he was nearly a sibling, so timid about the world he wouldn't go away even when let out. He perched on the fence and stared at her in a way that no boy had ever done. She knew her father watched over her as if she were also wounded— too vulnerable to leave the house or the yard, even though she was restless and always looking out a window or over the fence at the other houses. He confined her, so she talked to the owl. "It's our secret," she said, knowing her father would not allow it—if he actually heard what she said and saw the love in the owl's eyes. And sometimes the owl glanced at her as if to take hold of her body, as if he saw the fragile bones hidden inside her rough wings, as if he could breathe the delicate air in which she lived.

Abandoned Father

My daughter tilts her head back and shields her eyes from the sun. She has come looking for me, wanting me to come back to her, to hug her against my chest until she can close her eyes and forget my absence, until she can remember only how she rode on my shoulders, bobbing up and down, screaming with laughter. But I'm not the father she wants to remember. I'm the father who is fading from her eyes and memory, the father who rises into the clouds like a vapor from the drops of moisture on the grass, the father who will soon fall back to earth again in the heavy rains.

In Childhood

My neighbor Helene said I was born of a predatory bird like a red-tailed hawk or an eagle. She laughed, lying on her belly in her rubber pool, her wet black hair shiny like a crow's feathers. I ploughed the air around her, whapping her with my powerful wings. While she tried to get out of the pool, splashing and falling and yelling for help, arms covering her head, I hovered over her, threatening to thwack her some more if she got up again.

Her brother Joey rocked on the swing, drawing his name in the dirt with a toe. When he finally looked up, I stood over him. He said I was born of a skunk, and he could smell me clear across our yards. I barraged him with handfuls of pebbles and rocks. Before he could get to the house, I wrestled him to the ground, rubbing his face in the dirt. "Smell this," I said and sat on his face until he started crying. When I let him up, he ran to the house and washed his mouth out and yelled, "You're still a skunk-boy."

At school, Giselle told me I was born of a snake, so I wound her tightly into a spool and didn't let up until she cried, "I take it back." I hissed at her awhile and laughed, and she seemed to laugh too. I pulled her long blond braids and kissed her cheek. I thought all was forgiven. "I love you," I said and then she started pummeling me with her fists and wouldn't stop.

Gifted Sister

My oldest sister is gifted. When things break, she fixes them. Though often they still don't work, our parents beam with pride. Sometimes our gifted sister breaks things just to fix them. And our parents beam with pride even more, except when she breaks things like my father's electric razor or my mother's hand mixer or blow dryer. Our gifted sister causes glasses to spill their juice on my other sister and myself. We are not gifted, but we know when we're thirsty and wet.

There are mysteries we don't understand like why our pet turtle now has a crack in its shell, but the shell still holds together even though the turtle has fallen asleep; why we found a trail of tiny slivers of glass sparkling in the carpet; and why our gifted sister smashed our pet plastic amphibians against the linoleum tiles. "Don't worry," she said with great confidence, "I'm taking them to my hospital; they'll need surgery." "What hospital?" we asked. "Shh," she said. "Do you want mom and dad to find out?"

Sometimes, for no good reason, our gifted sister hurls a candy dish or a plate against the wall and runs into her room, slamming the door. Then our mother stops our father from going after her. "Wait until the storm dies down," she says. "Then talk to her." Nor do we understand why our gifted sister screams at our father behind a closed door while our father says harshly, something that sounds like "Now look..." and then, after much commotion, they come back to the living room together, our gifted sister, still with tears bright in her eyes, kissing everyone on the cheek. Our mother smiles at us with thin, tight lips as if she expects us to smile and swallow at the same time, as if we are all in on the secret of how difficult it must feel to be gifted.

Searching for the Bearded Dragon

When I went to the terrarium, Sam, our bearded dragon was not there. I had been gone only for a few hours and expected him to scoot up my leg or leap on my foot. "Don't look at me," Danielle said. "I can't watch Sam every second of the day. He's probably in some corner feasting on a spider." We did a quick search of our place, calling his name and finding tiny hills of guano, which we cleaned from the scuffed floor with a paper towel and Windex. Next. I pulled out a few thawed dead crickets from the refrigerator and lay them in Sam's favorite feeding place outside his terrarium. Still Sam didn't come to us. "Maybe a bird sat on the window ledge, and he freaked out and is hiding in a shoe or in some other place safe from the shadow of a bird." She didn't really like Sam, because he was smelly and left a mess everywhere, and the few times he sat on her shoulder, he pooped on it. But Sam and I had bonded instantly the day we bought him home from the pet store. You can't really train a bearded dragon, nor can you force them to love your lover. I got the flashlight with the high beam and began a thorough search of the house, checking our shoes, the pockets of our jackets and coats, all our drawers, the closets, the light fixtures, under the bed and the couch, but came up empty-handed. Then we returned to Sam's lush terrarium filled with fresh soil, green succulents, gravel, small trees, chia, plush mushroom rising like trees with red caps, shining crystals, figurines, a mini slide and tiny lights in the shape of stars. Sam was not in there. Danielle, placing her hand on my shoulder, called off the search. "I'm sure he's here somewhere, and he'll come out when he's ready," she said. "Let's just do what we normally do." *But what do we normally do*, I wondered, *and how could it be normal without Sam?* "It'll be okay," she said and kissed me on the lips.

Father Obscura

My mother woke up to a hole in her stomach, right where her bellybutton used to be, the day I was packing to leave for camp. She screamed. "Would you look at this, please!"

And then she was standing naked in my bedroom, pointing at it. Her boobs dangling, large and festive, like Macy's Parade floats. You could see all the way through her bellybutton to our backyard mess, the weeds that had taken over the garden. Through the hole in her stomach I could recognize my childhood baby doll, our runaway cat Sammy, and the faraway look on my father's face when he died of cancer.

"My God, it's dark," she said, her stomach heavy with ghosts.

Mom In the Kitchen

Mom stands in our checked kitchen, she's had so much coffee she looks insane. She gets through a busy day with ready-bake boxes, a checked apron, a wet, weird smile, and checked mixing bowls that nest inside each other like checked Russian Dolls. Her apron matches the kitchen, and the kitchen matches the dog, and the dog scoots along on his bottom on the matching checked throw rug. When her headache intensifies, she takes her pills. "It's a pain in the ass getting old," Mom says, and she means it. "Don't move," Mom says, and she means that too. I imagine sitting inside the warm oven—that's the way my childhood feels as if I'm about to be baked and eaten. I go back to playing with my limping dolls. I have given each of them an injury, "Easy does it," I say, before bandaging their legs.

Wig

The wig arrived in a pretty pink box. I'd ordered it online from a wig shop. Silky, blonde and long, it felt as if I were entertaining a movie star in my hallway. Grace Kelly in a box on my couch. "So nice to meet you," I said, slipping it on.

On my head, it looked a bit different, but I sashayed around the hallway naked, slipped on a shortie night shirt and long-nosed barracuda slippers, then waltzed myself into the living room. I sat on the sofa impressing the dog. A few hours later, I went to the mirror to remove it but it wouldn't come off. My husband came home, took one look at me and began unbuttoning his shirt. "God," he said, "is it Halloween? Take that thing off." I again tried to remove it, but it was stuck as if crazy glued to my scalp. I went to the bathroom mirror to see what I could do; all of the wig's elegance was gone. The weight of it pressed down on my face.

I thought about cutting the wig, but that wouldn't solve the problem. Instead, I stepped into the shower and turned the hot water on full blast, letting it splash over my face and head, hoping that the steam would loosen it enough to gently pull it off. After about twenty minutes, I wrapped a towel around myself and rubbed enough steam off the mirror to see myself. There was some gray in the wig now as there was in my own hair, but I was seeing something different, *I can do something with this,* I thought. Grace was gone and an unknown actress in her middle years, an actress who had featured in great character roles, had taken her place, bawdy and ready for a fight.

Later, my husband got over his caution and kissed my head. "Your hair smells good," he said. He rubbed his head against it as if it were our dog's soft coat. He blew gently through hairs as if trying to spread the sparks into logs that had not yet broken into flame. He felt like a stranger, with his greying chest hairs. "You're messing up my hair," I said and lit a French cigarette. He did what he always does when he wants to seduce me. He recited a poem from Pablo Neruda in his most alluring voice. And at last I told him what I had always wanted to tell him: "It's a bad translation."

Trolllikeness

One evening, just before dinner, the door lock clicked, and a troll entered our home. For a troll, he wasn't bad looking—lean and muscular, goat like, but without hooves or horns. "What are you doing here?" my sister asked. Walking past us, he sat down in the living room. "Pour me a drink," he ordered. "How did you get a key?" my sister asked. "I'm your father," he answered, "home at last." I scrutinized his face to see if there was any resemblance, but he didn't look like either of us. My sister ran out of the room and came back with a butcher knife, waving it at him. "You're a troll," she said. "You can't be our father." "Why not? You're half troll. Look in the mirror." My sister let the knife drop to her side. We walked to the mirror and looked at ourselves. We resembled each other. The troll came up behind us and put his arms around us. He smelled like a river and towered over us in the mirror. "Trolls stick together," he said hugging us so tightly we almost passed out and had no choice but to cry out, "Father."

Menopausal Mother

Mother was in menopause, but with her silk nightie on, she could still do anything with style. She'd sashay out of the kitchen and dance a bit—while baking brownies or banana pudding. She was growing a tail, but she wasn't mean. She'd yell, "I'm pulling a Houdini in here!" which was embarrassing, but it only meant she was adjusting to her screwy hormones. Only one boy was brave enough to visit. Shawn. I liked his sharpened features and the way his nose bent to the right. We were in deep. "Thickly hormonal," Mother called it. Sometimes she'd scowl at us and slam a few doors. I warned him about how, some days, she curled up on the kitchen floor to blow off a little steam.

Shawn wasn't worried. He pronounced Mother "elegant and other-worldly," suspected a ghost had stung her in some way. I cried because it sounded so true, but he said he had read that it was nearly epidemic with menopausal mothers. No need to worry or make a big deal of it. "I was just sayin' it can be a bit confusing," I said. "No joke."

"But she looks great in that nightie. Right?" Shawn said. I wasn't so sure. "What about the tail," I asked. "What tail?" he answered. Maybe he couldn't really see it.

I explained that she bought the nightie from a store downtown the week after Dad went off to Portugal to live with Selina, my former au pair. Shawn hadn't known about this until I told him, and I, until I voiced it, had not admitted it to myself. He commanded me to stop worrying about Mother. "Poodle piss! She still makes great banana Margaritas, doesn't she?"

For him, in fact, Mother made them every single day. Shawn enjoyed perching near her in the kitchen, sipping her

Margaritas, feeling the sun on his face. Sometimes, he'd hide behind the stove or wear her plush bedroom slippers. And Mother's curving tail…. It kept growing until she had to put on some jeans. She'd safety-pin it down so no one would notice. Sometimes it would slip out through a pocket, as if looking for something to sting, or to love.

Redundancy

After he was made redundant at work, Dad wore a pair of ratty cut-off jeans and a sailor's hat and walked around the house as if he were lost at sea. Often at night he stared out the window, waiting to spot the dog star, and when he did, he exclaimed, "Thar she is," as if he had suddenly found a purpose. But when Mom questioned him about why he was wandering around half naked or asked him to do something such as clean up around his study or take the garbage out or scrape off the dishes or even help out in the galley, peeling potatoes or washing greens, he snapped at her, "Treat me like an officer!"

Near Christmas my mother exploded. "Would you please see a doctor?" Mom insisted. The doctor diagnosed him with double depression. My mother said he was wired for it. "It's not one scoop," Mom told me. "It's a double, with sprinkles."

"He's not an ice cream sundae, Mom," I answered. But she did have a point. Whenever they spoke, there was a stuck daisy in my throat and the petals kept falling off. I wanted my mother to throw him a life raft and I wanted him to come back to himself before some scavenger could snatch what was left of his spirit. But every day, my mother pushed my father further into his dream, and every day, my father pushed off farther into the sea, waving a lantern without a light.

Kiss-Monger

Arthur is a natural ham, a kiss-monger. When he sees a lady, he'll pucker his lips. Other times he is a little explosion waiting to happen. What I'm saying is: this child can be tricky. He could set a fire on fire. He has tantrums the size of Florida. At such times, he's as unkissable as a dragon. But in public, he's the perfect grandson, smiling like a puppy and irresistible. I think about that lady who beelined toward my grandson, all smiles and warm heaving chest, all maternal love and nowhere to put it. "Kiss me," I should have said. "Kiss my cheeks, my tear stained lips, my dandy little hat." But all she saw was Arthur. And within an instant her lips were locked on his cheeks while he pinched her behind and she almost jumped out of her girdle. "That boy needs some manners," she shouted. "No one asked you to kiss him," I shouted back. I've constructed a little sign, to let the ladies know that he is not their property. Now when they pass us by, they look me in the eye. They see me for who I am, a well-preserved beauty, a caring grandmother! A woman who smells like holiday cookies all year round. A woman determined to ward off all kissers either by yanking them from his angelic face so that they almost rise off the ground or by swinging her cane. "I won't let them near you," I tell him, "so don't complicate things, please." Often he murmurs and puckers his lips as if to convince me of his good intentions, and I'm almost tempted to kiss him myself. "Let them kiss me," he says, bouncing up and down like an angry cantaloupe.

Snapping Turtle

On our video call, my son told me he found a snapping turtle baby in a nearby creek. "Why were you at a creek in this weather, and what were you doing that you spotted a baby snapping turtle?" Since he was little he was always climbing to the highest branch of a tree, or skateboarding down a hill at night, pushing the limits. He ignored my questions and held it up in his hand. "They're illegal here," he said proudly. The snapping turtle inched along his palm, grazing on skin. "What do you plan to do with it when it gets snappier?" I asked. "One day your pet will be able to take a big chunk out of your leg." The snapping turtle looked at me with his cute prehistoric face as if to say, "Can it, granny. I've got a good deal. I'm not going to blow it." "Mom, don't be so melodramatic," he said. "Herbie already loves me. And isn't he adorable?" He was cute like a toy version of a tyrannosaurus rex. "What are you feeding it?" I asked. "Raw chicken." "What are you going to do with Herbie when he turns into a killer?" "He'll stay here with me," he said, "and he won't kill anything." I didn't say anything else. I was looking out the window, keeping an eye out for my weekly ride to the doctor. "Ouch," he said as Herbie nipped the skin on his palm. He detached the critter and held him upside down to the camera. If looks could kill, I thought. "He's helpless really," my son said, and then my camera froze.

House Full of Dust

As I touched my husband, he turned to dust. The cup he'd been drinking from became a bit of fluff. "This makes sense," my mother said to me, goddess of failed marriages. "Be happy." "Happy about what?" I said, but it was never a good idea to argue with my mother. In truth, I actually liked him better as a dust bunny. He was less threatening and what he lost in human proportion, he gained in charm. The house was full of the dust of old lovers who had long ago drifted. And now he was joining the others. "What a mess," I said to nobody. Who will come over with a broom? And will I ever find a lover who will not turn into some kind of particulate? Mom shook her head. Her scalp was no longer balding and patchy, now more like a mushroom of glowing light. "You never learned how to be alone," she said. Lint floated in the still air between us, making it hard not to sneeze her away. "I like men," I said. "You like dust," she answered. She had a point. I wanted so much to hug her and tell her she has always been right about me. And then, she was gone. But a little ball of gray wool fuzz clung to my sweater. I picked it off gently with my two fingers and blew it into the air.

Nose Job

After the swelling had gone down and her eyes were no longer blood-shot, after she could look in the mirror and not see herself as a human bruise, my sister returned to school happy with her new nose, which was cute and pert, perky in fact. She no longer looked sad and unrecognizable. Her cheeks were shiny and unique, and she greeted everyone with a memorable smile and received congratulations. Some of her girlfriends said that she looked beautiful like a movie star and others admired the fine craftsmanship from a distance. For the most part, the boys stayed away. But then, as the weeks went by and the nose was no longer fragile, it began to receive another kind of attention. Boys pressed it repeatedly and made dinging sounds. Girls fiddled with it as if it were a loose button. One boy touched it gently and offered her a Mickey Mouse ring. And even her teacher couldn't resist, pinching it. "It's so so *you*," she said peering down at her over wire-rims. Soon, the nose became sore and swollen again. "Why am I cursed?" my sister, almost in tears, asked her nose. All stuffy, her nose replied, "I'll leave you noseless if you don't put an end to all of this nose-loving." And then one day, when a boy in her class rang her nose repeatedly, she punched his nose, breaking it right in the middle. The boy needed a nose job to repair the damage, and she knew exactly where to send him. Later, she broke the teacher's nose by accident, and she broke the nose of the most beautiful girl in class, blood all over the place. This was how my sister, with her wonderful new nose, became famous.

A Birthday Wish

I closed my eyes and made a wish before I blew out the one stubborn candle on my cup cake. "Ouch," I said. Of course, my friends knew I didn't like cupcakes. They laughed and handed me colorful wrapped bars of dark chocolate, the kind I wasn't allowed to eat anymore. "What did you wish for?" they asked. "At our age, it's okay to tell." But I kept my wish secret, putting my finger to my lips and shaking my head. My wish floated out the window, becoming unrecognizable. Its blotchy wings caught the sunlight as it slouched on a branch, sighing and closing its feathers, body slender as a thread. I squinted my eyes to see it better, but my eyes didn't like being asked to do anything at their age. My friends blinked into the dim afternoon light. "Tell us your wish," they insisted, as though my wish were somehow important to their future. A gust of wind swept through, followed by another gust. Sun sparkled on a swarm of gnats rising from the ground. Whatever wish I wished had vanished from my memory.

Family Sorcerer

Under the evening star of the Winter Solstice, I persuaded an evil sorcerer into undoing the curse on my family. One brother escaped the sticky web of indecision in which he'd been caught like a fly since college. He stood there beaming at me with his contagious smile. The other brother pushed away the boulder that had crushed his legs in middle age and leaped up like a gymnast and told us about his exciting escape. Then, after years, my mother flew up out of a pile of ashes. "You're all such successes!" she chirped. We held hands and laughed, and one of the brothers told the old family joke about Cousin Mildred, who fell in the bathtub, her head cracking open like a watermelon. "And then Mildred became a concert pianist," my mother reminded us. "Before the fall in the bathtub, she could hardly play Three Blind Mice."

We toasted Cousin Mildred and second chances. One of my brothers did a funny impression of our father, who had run off to Hollywood when we were little to become an actor. "Remember his bad Fred McMurray impression?" my brother said. It was amazing to be back together like this, but something was bothering me. The evil sorcerer kept quiet, but I could feel him brooding. I could see something foreboding in his large brown eyes. "I'm worried," I said to the sorcerer, pulling him aside. I noticed that the sorcerer's hat was frayed around the edges and then for a moment his face changed. It was our father. "Dad?" I said, staring into the patched elbows of his sweater. "Shh!" he said, his skin as wrinkled as the milk skim on an old cup of burnt coffee. "Only you can see me as I am. Don't tell them," he said. "It's HIM!" I shouted. Immediately, my siblings began arguing, their faces cracking with anger. My mother confronted her husband. "What did you do to us?" she demanded to know. "I brought you together," he said, "then and now." "You ruined us," she said, and then, before our mother could punch him, the sorcerer disappeared. A cold wind blew through the room as she dissolved into a swirl of ashes. For a moment, my brothers stopped fighting and stared into the small tornado that was our mother. Then the first evening star blinked out, and a blanket of tiny indifferent stars spread over the sky like a net.

Fatherless Daughters

In Springtime, abandoned daughters burst like myopic butterflies with binoculars attached to their faces while they try to identify their absent fathers, who zip through the clouds like geese, but they're not geese, and they have no sense of direction. "Can you see me down here, Dad?" one abandoned daughter trills, while one father zigzags ever closer to the sun. "It's hurting my eyes," he yells waving his pale wings like flags. Another abandoned daughter spots a cloud in the shape of her father and flies through him again and again. "He wasn't much of a father," she says. "He's better as a cloud." Another daughter shouts, "Heads up!" as her father falls from the sky headlong into the crowd of abandoned daughters. The other fathers cringe and avoid looking down. "They're out to get us," they say. "They want money or hugs or something." The daughters, tired of treading air, fling themselves toward their fathers, eager to bring one home, even if he's someone else's father, even if he never earns another dime, even if he sheds all his feathers—but the fathers prove illusive, no longer really fathers.

Section 6

House of Grana Padano

The Grana Padano House of Wedgewood

My husband's ex lives in a house made of cheese, catty corner from a grocery. She moved to Wedgewood only a short while ago. She is so attractive that even women blush when they see her, and men follow her like homeless dogs. "Why did she move here?" I ask my husband. He pretends that he doesn't know what I'm talking about. "I haven't seen her in years," he answers. Wherever I am, his ex appears. If I'm picking out avocados, she's standing behind me. If I'm in the dress shop, she'll walk out of the dressing room in a long blue dress and stare at herself in the mirror while the men peer in the windows. If I drive up to the bank teller, she's at the ATM drive up. I can't get away from her. She's the talk of Wedgewood, and her house is lovely and delicious in the way that a wheel of Grana Padano cheese is. When I say "delicious," I mean it, as I have taken to secretly breaking off little chunks and eating them on my walks through the town. When I ask my husband if he's talked with his ex-wife, he always responds the same way. "Are you still obsessed with her?" I'm not obsessed with her. Still, despite his denials and criticism, every evening I go for my walk and nibble a little more of her house.

The Smell of the Ex

My husband's ex smells like Hawaiian flowers. She moved to our village only a short while ago, but I see her all over town, local men trailing behind her. Whenever I say anything about it, my husband says I'm obsessed. "What a ridiculous assertion," I say. "Maybe you're obsessed." I wink, trying to reduce the tension. But the truth is that his ex smells so damn wonderful that when she passes by me on the way to the grocery store, I can't help but follow just to inhale her. I've started to feel like her happy little homeless dog. "Remind me why she moved here again?" I ask. He doesn't answer but begins sniffing all around the living room. "Do you smell Grana Padano somewhere in the living room," he asks. "What are you talking about," I reply. "I'm going out for avocados." I close my eyes and head for the grocery store as if blind, but everywhere I go, I smell Hawaiian flowers.

The Nervous Little Wife

No matter where I go here in Wedgewood, my ex-husband's wife goes with me, following me to the avocados in the grocery and peeking through the curtain when I try on the long blue dresses at the vintage dress shop. She is so small and nervous that I'd like to cup her in my hands and feed her bits of parmesan cheese.

When I see my ex, he pretends that he doesn't see me, even if we pass shoulder to shoulder on the street. I've gotten used to it. However, once I did stop him right in front of the grocery. "Your strange little wife seems to be following me," I said. "Why are you obsessed with her?" he asked. And then I noticed the crumbled Grana Padano deep within his beard.

Mistaking One Cheese for Another

She said her house was Grana Padano, but it was really Pecorino. I'm not a snob or anything about cheeses but who goes around boasting about her house being made of cheese and then gets it wrong. It's hard to know what to say to her. So, I sniff around her house at night when she's sleeping and pinch the corners. It crumbles into my palm. "Pecorino," I say to myself and take a plastic container home for my husband to sample. "Yes," he says. "Only my ex would mistake Pecorino Romano for Grana Padano. But then again, her pasta was always mushy and not even a good Pecorino can help that." He tastes the cheese again and licks his lips. Now he's eating the cheese and saying that's it got a wonderful flavor. And I can only imagine that the flavor reminds him of her, salty and buttery, like some kind of sheep mulling through the grasses, its body full of curls.

Near Collision on Main Street

The second wife nearly collided with her husband's ex-wife on Main Street. The new wife was carrying a small bag of avocados, and her husband's ex held a clear plastic bag with a blue dress. They looked at each for a long moment before the second wife said, "Excuse me," politely and started to walk past, but the ex stopped her by holding up her hand and flicking her long thin fingers up and down. "Since we always seem to be in the same place at the same time, we may as well get along," she said. "I agree with that," the second wife said, "But why did you move back to Wedgewood?" "I grew up here," she said, "And I love the Grana Padano cheese." The second wife noted how rosy her cheeks were and the fleshiness of her lips. She squinted her eyes to block out the bright sun. "My husband says you're still obsessed with him." The ex chuckled and motioned for the second wife to follow her across the street, leading her to her own house, which was made of Grana Padano cheese. She pointed to the places where chunks had been bitten off. And now the second wife understood why her husband always had bits of Grana Padano in his beard. She also couldn't help noticing that the ex-wife had a perfect ass. With all the cheese she probably eats too, the second wife thought, it's got to be genetic.

Kissing Grana Padano

She comes home with a shopping bag from the dress shop, a chip on her shoulder, and dots of cheese on her lower lip, cheek and in her hair. I kiss her lips lightly. It's Grana Padano. I swipe her cheek and lick it from my fingertip, very salty. Then I brush it out of her hair. "Some reason you're kissing me before dinner," she asks. "No reason. I just like to kiss you no matter what time of day or night." But she knows I'm attempting to divert her from the inevitable question. "I saw your ex again. Why did she move here?" "If you go to her house, you are likely to see her," I say. Her question goes unanswered as I sit down on the couch and pick up my iPad to read the news. But it's difficult to concentrate with her glowering at me. The sun is going down behind the chip on her shoulder. Finally, I answer. "I don't think of her as my ex anymore. I don't think of her at all. I have a sexy beautiful wife to keep me occupied." She beams a smile full of sky streaked with red, violet, pink. Then she straddles me and kisses me repeatedly, content for now with my answer. I kiss her lips, her chin, her neck. She smells and tastes of Grana Padano, which again reminds me of my ex.

It Wasn't Really Blue

It was neither parmesan, nor pecorino; it may not even have been Grana Padano; but it was a house, a house of Grana Padano. It was not the ex-wife of a boyfriend or part-time lover, it was her husband's ex wife who lived there. And it was not just *an* ex-wife of her husband, it was the one and only ex-wife of her one and only husband. "Wasn't there another town she could have moved to?" the wife asked. "After all, she's not just your ex; she's your only ex." It wasn't a sunny day, nor was it cloudy, and she didn't mind the smell of Grana Padano that trailed her husband everywhere he went. Why did that smell permeate his clothing?

She didn't think it important that she try on a blue dress that day, but she went to the dress shop to try one on anyway. She certainly wasn't obsessed with her husband's ex, but the ex seemed to be everywhere she went, and was now in the dress shop, looking adorable in a jogging outfit that didn't actually cover her ass.

The second wife was trying on a blue dress that, as it turned out, wasn't really blue, nor was it adorable like the ex's jogging outfit. It wasn't smart either. But it was a dress— a beautiful gray or avocado green. But what if it wasn't right on her? She didn't want to ask her husband's ex what to think, but she did so anyway; *why not?* she thought. It was never bad to have another woman's opinion. They may not be friends but they don't have to be enemies either. "Do you mind if I ask you how I look in this dress?" "Hm," her husband's ex said, "not bad, though blue is probably not your color." "But the dress is not really blue," the second wife said. "Exactly," the ex-wife replied and walked out of the dress shop, leaving behind a fine dusting of cheese.

Didn't We See Her?

2nd Wife: why did she move here?

Husband: Did she actually move here? And how do we know she moved here?

2nd Wife: How do we know she didn't? Didn't we see her again today?

Husband: Did we? If we did see her, how do we know it was really her?

2nd Wife: Who else dresses like her in this town? Who else wears that long blue dress?

Husband: You're asking me who else dresses like her? Have I ever seen her in a long blue dress?

2nd Wife: Didn't you see her today? And wasn't she wearing a long blue dress?

Husband: Was it even blue? Or was it turquoise? And was that her in the dress?

2nd wife: Who else would it be? Who else would weave up and down the block, swaying her ass like a duck shaking water out of its tail feathers? Who else would walk around town with a wedge of Grana Padano in her hands?

Husband: Was that Grana Padano or parmesan? Are you saying she's nutty?

2nd Wife: Are you saying she isn't?

Husband: Why do you think you keep seeing her?

2nd Wife: Why do you think you don't see her?

Husband: Isn't this conversation embarrassing?

2nd wife: Why would I be embarrassed? And what's wrong with this conversation?

Husband: Who said anything was wrong?

Like

She was like a handful of fireflies, like a snow of feathers floating over Main Street. She moved like a blue dress waltzing under the moon to something like music or perhaps it was like a soft wind. She spread her wings like a swan, shaking off crumbles of Grana Padano cheese. She was like something delicious everyone wants to nibble. She was like a mist bandaging the eyes of her blind ex, who couldn't even see that she was everywhere like dust particles lit by rays of light. She was like the tall trees blocking the view of the forest. She was like a sudden enchantment catching everyone in its net. But the second wife could see through her like a two-way mirror; on the other side, she wouldn't say why she had come here, and the interrogation kept repeating itself like someone with a stutter.

Section 7

Cognac Dream

Wolf Hybrids

My husband's ex-wife moved to our small town and brought five wolf hybrids with her. She would glide through town with the wolf hybrids pulling in front of her as though she were on a sled. When people saw her coming, they got out of the way or crossed the street to walk on the other side.

Tall and beautiful, she smiled at everyone as she passed, but the wolf hybrids, unlike dogs, stared out with deep brown eyes that were unwilling to make a connection or engage others. They often snarled at those who tried to offer a treat or get near them. I admired the fluidity of their movements, their thick coats, and long legs. They didn't seek approval.

To my surprise, when I'd get near them, they held my gaze for a long moment as if they recognized me as a kindred spirit. Perhaps it was only my imagination. I looked directly at them, but not at my husband's ex-wife, who never spoke a word to me.

My husband's ex kept her house spare with only a strange looking avocado couch, a few chairs, an ostrich lamp, and walls covered with photos of her wolf hybrids. When walking by, I'd peek in her living room window. My husband never spoke of her.

Once I asked him, "Why did she move here?" "Maybe to get to know you a little better," he answered. Gloom filled our home for the rest of the day while he sulked and mumbled to himself, but the next morning, he was cheery, preparing a spinach omelet with toast and jam and home fries. I never asked him again.

They say wolf hybrids can hear sounds at great distances and can predict the future. One night, I went to her house and saw that the wolf hybrids were not chained in her yard.

They prowled as if looking for prey. They began howling, but as I approached, they became silent. "Why are you here," I asked. "Why is she here?"

They moved together facing me as if forming a battle line. They didn't answer unless silence was their answer. I felt as if I were standing on the edge of a cliff, with nowhere else to go and them in pursuit—until the largest of the wolf hybrids broke ranks and pressed her snout against the fence sniffing me until she knew all she needed to know.

Cognac Dream

In the dream, my husband was screaming while being eaten alive by five wolf hybrids. His screams were muffled by the wolf hybrid sitting on his face. They were devouring his body slowly, focusing first on his shins and thighs. I was in the dream too, but I floated in the air like a body made of dust. Just as the wolf hybrids devoured my husband's whole body, and a wind swept through me, splitting me apart, I woke up.

"I've got to stop drinking cognac at night," I said to myself, pacing the bedroom, wondering where on earth my husband might be. I looked under the bed, I looked in the closet. I opened the curtains to see if he might be sitting outside, which he often did these days, as if waiting for visitors to arrive. I examined my husband's section of the bed carefully; it was still warm, but there was a chunk of gray wolf-hybrid fur near his pillow. I walked outside under the streetlamps to see if I could find him in one of the shops or bars on Main Street. But he was not in any of them, though I could smell his acrid scent lingering in the places where he must have been.

And then I saw his ex-wife coming toward me with her team of wolf hybrids. Before I could say anything, she disappeared. I kept walking on Main Street until it ended and I found myself in field near the edge of the forest. A wolf hybrid howled from within the forest. I followed the sound, thinking my husband may have gone out on a trail with his flashlight. Somewhere in the middle of the woods, I encountered a wolf hybrid, looking at me with greedy yellow eyes, licking his chops, a pile of white bones on the ground in front of him.

Catching the Future

I lured a crow into a trap with a dead vole. Before he could fly off, the cage fell over him. The crow pressed into the bars but couldn't slip through. I covered the cage with a blanket and carried it home. When I removed the blanket, the crow, hunkered down in the corner, let out a volley of shrill cries, so I covered the cage again until there was silence. When I lifted the blanket this time, the crow said, "What do you want?"

"The future," I said. "How long will I live?"

Sizing me up with his large deep eyes, the crow prophesied bad luck ahead, describing in detail all the possible ways I might die as punishment for his captivity and then repeating everything over and over like a parrot.

"You might be crushed by your lover in bed; you might be hit by a falling coconut; a clown might swing you by your ankles knocking your head against a wooden post until you are senseless, etc."

"If I let you go," I asked, "will you promise not to curse me?"

"Anything can happen," he said.

I lifted the cage and opened the window. After he flew away, I lay down among the piles of black feathers, afraid for my future and too tired to clean up the mess.

Sneaker Wave

Each day she was more like a mermaid. Sitting near the windowsill, waiting for the Weeki Watchee men.

Distrusting the sea, her mother was surprised, worried that her daughter had a mermaid calling. But she looked at her mother's coffee table, strewn with chemotherapy survival packets and old women's magazines, never a word about a fin or a tail.

"Don't be snide," she muttered at her mother under her sea breath. Since her mother got sick, she kept the mean words to herself. The Weeki Watchee uncles, a middle-aged carload, would be here any minute to take her to her inauguration. Tammy, a blonde pole-dancer, last year's mermaid, would hand her the trophy and pose with her next to the pedestal.

The sounds of the sea had followed her the day she first walked into the lodge, when she felt how sick she was as a human. She floated into the meeting, water coming down from her eyes as her fins moved around. Then one of the uncles came over and propped her up—she was just the right size and had, miraculously, landed on their beach.

'That was a sneaker wave,' he said.

She was done with being part of the herd, an ordinary high school girl. Her uncles brought her glasses of cucumber water or poured it over their own heads, just to make her laugh.

"They're sincere, Mom," she said with her pooling eyes. She tried not to worry about the human cancer stalking her mother. Instead, she dreamed about crawling into a shell, living there quietly, while the big changes happened around her. Inside the shell, she would glow from the inside out, drinking seawater slowly, looking back at the ways she might easily have drowned.

Quaking

I'm at the sink, the house is quaking, and I'm tired of being a wife. "The bills still need to be paid," I shout. My husband, from the back of the house, yells back at me that he always pays on time, but then why do we keep getting debt notices by text and email? The house is shaking, shimmy shammying, cha-cha-chaing like something out of a cartoon—and my husband reminds me of a cartoon bird with a curved beak and an appetite for sarcasm. It's difficult to stand with the house in constant motion, even though I hold on to the table. I feel the way my mother must have felt when she swore she saw my father's ghost, floating through the kitchen in the late evenings. The windows are starting to break. "What are we going to do?" I shout. My husband is either trying to get to me or attempting to escape the house. Plaster falls over us, his hair and face white. The dog is under the table where we should be. I point at the dog, my mouth saying "good dog" with admiration in my voice. Now the ceiling is coming down in chunks. "We're dying," my husband shouts. And I yell back, "That'd be a relief," though maybe he's right. And then the whole damn place collapses. When the quaking stops, we all dig our way out. The dog emerges from the rubble and shakes off the plaster dust. My husband rises, but he's not so clean. He hugs me tightly and that feels good, but then I push myself back. "Next month," I say, "pay the bills on time."

Dad With Porpoise

The year your mother drowned, your father claims she became a porpoise. He would drive you to the beach where you'd both try and spot her. "They're hardly ever visible here," he'd say, binoculars swinging from his neck.

You remember the day it snowed on the Pacifica beach when you were four years old. Flakes melted the second they hit sand. Your mother picked you up and twirled you in her arms. "Your father claims it never snows here," she laughed.

You hope your mother is smiling inside the water because when she was human, her face didn't do that. He said that she wasn't even very far out in the ocean the last time he saw her arcing. One day, she leapt right onto his boat. "There are hardly any photos of your mother on land."

He seems unaware of your weightlessness—how living without a mother has made you too light to matter. Your breasts, which seem to have decided not to come out, dip like sinkholes in your chest.

In your mind, there is a photo of your father on his boat holding a porpoise in his lap. The porpoise has leapt from the water and accidentally landed right there in his boat. Even though the porpoise is stuck there, it doesn't look sad. When you look at it, it's easy to believe that wonderful things can still happen. Your father reassures you about your mother's safety in the ocean, that porpoises are terrific at hiding from sharks. He says their low frequency sounds keep them from bumping into trouble. "One of these times…" he says, his milky eyes quiet. Sometimes, you worry that he's going to fall asleep on you.

There are dangers in having an intelligence nobody believes in. The kind that is questionable, like snow in Pacifica. "I'm not going to hold my breath," you say, holding it anyway.

No Rescue

Today, the pharmacist is shouting back at a woman at the counter, "We don't have the vaccine, please check the website!" She twitches as though she has been struck. Behind her the line collapses as she skitters off into the long vitamin aisle on the way to the exit. At home, your bored teenager shoots his bb gun at the birds, laughing until they begin shooting back. He hides in the bushes, as the bbs pockhole the front window. Now the birds are the ones laughing. Last night, your sister called to say she's no longer interested in being your sister and that being your sister has been the single worst thing in her life, "Don't call me your sister again," she screamed. The sun burns up the graves in the street, leaving piles of ash and houses with socially distanced mourners. Your dog coughs, his stomach wobbles and you can barely pull him out of the driveway. The cat ran away six months ago, tired of being called "Puss" and the predictable dinner menu. You are so used to wearing a mask you forget to take it off at home. When you look in the mirror, you think you are actually better looking with only half of your face peeking out. When you close your eyes and touch your wife's sanitized skin, it is like touching air.

Looking for a Light

"The dope here is really dope," my wife says and lies back down on her rug, her lips glistening like wet pearls, like clamshells puckering in sand—white paper stuck between them. She's been stoned ever since the night she came home from the hospital. And now we have a house full of dopes and mooches—her new friends— and a back porch on fire with red sun. "Pour me a Manhattan," she says. We don't have the ingredients to make a Manhattan. I walk into the kitchen, figuring she'll forget about it before I return. Out in the garden, her friends are pulling red apples off our tree. The tree looks empty and sad. A few of the women hold on to their apples, their hands filled with little red balls, as though they have the idea that they are lucky. I come back with an apple and no drink. My wife's beautiful eyes stare out as though she's having some kind of vision. I place the apple in her hand, but it slips out and rolls on the floor. A stranger with a scraggly beard comes in asking for a light. "Who invited you," I reply and send him away unlit and full of dust, though he claims someone greater is meeting him here, and it would be best not turn him away. "You should have let him stay. He might have been waiting for Jesus," she says with a sneer and then passes out. I carry her upstairs and lay her down in the bed. The house clears out except for the smoke. There are still a few women in the yard topless and praying to the apple tree—for what, I don't know. When Jesus arrives, he's also looking for a light and a free joint, but I send him away and lock the door.

Dream Retrieval

After getting laid off for the fourth time, Bob left the house only to take the dog on long walks on trails where he wouldn't encounter anyone else. He would spend days on the sofa talking to the dog. "You and your dog," I said. "OUR dog," Bob answered, stroking her behind her ears, kissing her nose, telling her about all of the things he had once hoped to do. "Sunsets are like Jackson Pollacks," Bob used to say. "They need to express themselves." But he always confused Pollock with DeKooning, and he actually meant Rothko. The two of them, Bob and our dog, made such a picture together, like a children's story—if Bob were a child—sitting near the living room window, watching the sun dip into a sea of grass or a bird plunge toward a field mouse or vole. "Bob, are you ever going to look for a job again?" I would ask, and he would always answer, "When I'm thirty again." On the way out the door for the late shift at the diner, I would spritz my neck with musk, but Bob wouldn't even turn his head. The dog caught the scent of my perfume and would jump off the couch and come over to sniff me and lick me good bye. He looked so happy to see me in my diner outfit, tail wagging and eyes bright, as if he was hoping I would give him a break from Bob. In the early morning hours, finally in bed, I imagined new ways to break it off with Bob, though I knew he would never leave me. "Go get it," Bob would shout in his sleep, as if he thought I would retrieve his youth, and as always, the dog leaped on our bed and licked him awake.

Snail Women

The women were large as giant snails and round as moons. They lolled in and asked my husband for money. He did not know them but I had a feeling he would be nice to them. They were women, and they had breasts.

Between the two round women and myself, there were five breasts in the room, and one fake breast. The fake breast was an implant. I had named her "Iris." Iris is a beautiful name, it is the name of a blond woman running through a field of flowers, barefoot.

The two plump women moved in so close I could smell their shampoo. One of the women said to my husband that her breasts were as round as money. How much money would he pay her to touch them? My husband looked at me like a naughty dog might look at its master.

"Would you like to start with one nipple?" she said.

I realized that she did not see me there, in the room, with my lovely false breast, and my less-lovely real breast. The real breast did not have a name, which suddenly felt unfair. The other woman (less round) slid off her jeans. She didn't even ask if it would be okay. She had long legs. My husband's Adam's apple moved. He looked like a little boy lost in a huge grocery store. I found myself enjoying the fact that the round women had eye problems and could not see me standing there right in front of everything.

If I really wanted to speak to them, I could. I could even say, "go away now, ladies, this fella is married," but there was no reason to. I wanted to watch. To see if he could perform under such conditions.

I nudged his foot with my index finger and he flicked it off like lint. I touched his hair, whispered, "It is getting so long now..." and he shuddered. The other woman was watching, taking notes. The rounder woman with the kissing problem kept going.

My husband's eyes were fixed on the window. This made me sad, as though he were looking for me but couldn't find me.

It made me shiver all the way into the woods, where I slept with a pack of wild dogs—unseen.

Dead Bugs and Lovers

Yesterday, I tripped over a familiar young woman lying on the sidewalk and almost fell. "Watch where you're walking," the young woman said in a less than friendly tone. "What are you doing there?" I asked. "You could get hurt or cause someone to have a really bad spill." "I'm resting," she said. She had a bright ready smile. Men and women walked around us unconsciously like a wave moving around two large rocks in a stream. I reached my hand down to help her up, but she said she was fine and invited me to lie down with her. A few pigeons were hopping toward her, but I shooed them away. Then I lay down with her in the bright sun on a very busy sidewalk. Our conversation became intimate quickly. She told me that her ex-lover—a man who ate dead bugs for a living—had left her penniless after months of sitting on a blanket with an empty coin cup. "He collected buckets of dead bugs and stored them in the living room," she said. "Not so bad," I said. "Many people consider bugs a delicacy." I told her that I had left my ex-lover penniless with our 40 cats and now I was penniless, but happy to have my solitude. I noticed some cat fur on her black jeans and the silky soft hair on her arms. We talked about things we had in common, afternoon naps with large cats, a fear of growing old alone, the belief in bad luck that might change one into a toad or take away the ability to love. She rose to her feet and so did I. "Is it time to go?" I asked. "Yes, I think so," she said. She pecked me on the cheek, and I kissed her on the forehead. Then we kissed on the lips. "Your lips taste very sweet and familiar. Do I know you?" she said. "Yes, I'm your ex-lover," I said. I pulled a handful of dead bugs out of my pocket to prove it. Then we promised never to become ex-lovers again and went our separate ways.

Out of the Hat

I pulled my ex-husband out of one of my hats, and at first, he seemed happy to see me again. "I've really missed your hats, and all of your weird scarves," he said to me, beaming.

I contemplated stuffing him back into the hat, but then I remembered our days in Kansas City, how we used to split a package of Hostess cupcakes in the movie theater, and he'd always lick the vanilla cream out with his tongue before eating the cake part. I threw my arms around him, squishing him around the middle. He seemed to be filled with something I'd been living without for too long. He smelled like chocolate cake, and he had become portly. I licked his soft sweet cheeks and tasted his caramelly kisses. "I still have a sweet tooth," I admitted, shaking off my magic hat, unwinding my poppy-red scarf as the room heated up. Sunlight poked in through the blinds, my eyes watered, and it was becoming hard to see who was really there with me. Despite his efforts to stop me, I licked and kissed some more, and pretty soon, he was an amorphous bundle of crumbs. "Do you still love me," he said, so quietly that it was impossible to tell who was talking. "What a strange question," I replied. And with the dry pads of my fingers, I pinched little bits of him back inside my hat.

About Meg Pokrass

MEG POKRASS is the award-winning author of 8 flash fiction collections and 2 flash novellas, including *Spinning to Mars* (Blue Light Book Award, 2021) and *The Loss Detector* (Bamboo Dart Press, 2020). Her work has appeared in over 900 literary journals has been anthologized in 3 Norton anthologies: *Flash Fiction International* (W.W. Norton, 2015), *New Micro: Exceptionally Short Fiction* (W.W. Norton, 2018), and *Flash Fiction America* (W. W. Norton & Co., 2023). She is the Series Co-Editor of *Best Microfiction* and Founding Editor of *New Flash Fiction Review*. Meg lives in Inverness Scotland.

http://www.megpokrass.com

About Jeff Friedman

JEFF FRIEDMAN is the author of eight previous collections of poems, prose poems, and micros including *The Marksman*, *Floating Tales* and *Pretenders*. Friedman's work has appeared in *American Poetry Review, Poetry, New England Review, Poetry International, Cast-Iron Aeroplanes That Can Actually Fly: Commentaries from 80 American Poets on their Prose Poetry, 101 Jewish Poets of the Third Millennium, Flash Fiction Funny, Flash Nonfiction Funny, Fiction International, and The New Republic, and Best Microfiction 2021 and 2022.* He has received numerous awards, including a National Endowment Literature Translation Fellowship in 2016 and two individual Artist Grants from New Hampshire Arts Council.

https://poetjefffriedman.com

112 Harvard Ave #65
Claremont, CA 91711 USA

pelekinesis@gmail.com
www.pelekinesis.com

Pelekinesis titles are available through Small Press Distribution, Baker & Taylor, Ingram, Bertrams, and directly from the publisher's website.